I MISS POPPY

Cover & Interior Design: Lord's Image Designs

Copyright © 2021 by Denise S. Millben

Published by Lord's Image Publishing

Muncie, IN 47305

kizmin.jones@lordsimage.com

ISBN 978-0-9984160-1-4 (paperback)
Library of Congress Cataloging-in-Publication Data

Names: Millben, Denise S., author I Davis, Tashema, illustrator
Subject: LCSH: Christian life-Juvenile literature, Grief-Juvenile literature, Death-Juvenile literature
Description: First edition. Muncie, Indiana: Lord's Image [2021]

Printed in the United States of America
2021

I MISS POPPY

In loving memory of
S. Michael Millben
aka our "Poppy"

I'm only four years old but I need to tell you how I feel.

Today my grandpa died.

I am going to try to explain it for you.

My grandpa was a really nice man, but he was kind of old and he had a bald head.

He played with me and let me sit on his lap while he looked at motorcycles on his computer.

He would tickle me and my brother.

We called him Poppy. When Poppy sat down for dinner he always prayed.

He always looked nice, that was because he was a pastor, I guess.

Well, one day my dad and mom told me that Poppy was sick. He had something called cancer.

We tried our very best to do what dad and mom said, but sometimes we forgot.

I never noticed at first, but he was staying in his big chair and later in the bed more and more.

Gammy, my grandmother, got him a special bed that lifted his head up so he could see us better.

Every time I went into his room, I would say, "Hi Poppy" and he would say," hi baby." I am not a baby, but I did not say anything to him about it.

I do not remember a lot because adults keep important things from kids.

They think we cannot handle it.

That may be true for some kids but not me.

When Poppy came home, he looked great!

I was glad to see that he was up walking around.

We had family pictures taken and Poppy was smiling and making sure all our shirts were straight.

Family ♡

Then one day he wanted to see us in his room. He kissed us and Gammy was crying.

I wondered why she was crying? No one ever said. So, I guessed she just was not happy that day.

Grownups should talk to kids or we might start making up stories that are not right.

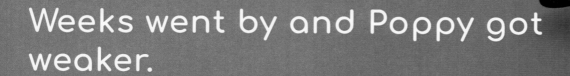

Weeks went by and Poppy got weaker.

One day Gammy was making Poppy a milkshake, she said it would help give him energy. It looked so good because it had a banana, chocolate almond milk and powder in it and I asked if I could have some.

She poured a little in a glass and when I drank it, yuck! It was nasty. I asked Gammy what was wrong with the shake and she told me that it did not have any sugar in it because Poppy could not have sugar.

I never asked for another one of his drinks.

In our family we all get together for Thanksgiving. I really like it when we all go to Poppy and Gammy's house.

There is a lot of food on the table and we all have to say what we are thankful for.

It must be worse than a cold or a sore throat because he was in the hospital at least three times. Then he and my Gammy went to Mexico to help him get better.

My mom went for a while too.

It seemed like they were gone forever.

When we went to his house to visit, we were told not to talk loudly or run through the house.

He needed peace and quiet.

Poppy is usually the one to get things started but this time he came out of the room using a walker.

We were thankful that he could walk.

He did not eat at the table with us. Gammy took his dinner into the room and he ate there. I thought he was getting better.

Then one Sunday evening, our whole family was at my Poppy and Gammy's house. The kids were in the family room watching a movie and suddenly all the adults left the room and went into their bedroom.

They made us kids stay in the family room.

I wanted to know what was going on.

When I looked around everyone was crying.

My mom was crying, my dad was crying, my uncles were crying, my aunts were crying, my big cousins were crying and my Gammy was crying.

Then my dad came and got me and my brother and took us into the room where Poppy was sleeping.

I thought we better be quiet because Poppy is asleep. I looked at him and he looked so calm and peaceful.

So why was everyone crying if Poppy is sleeping?

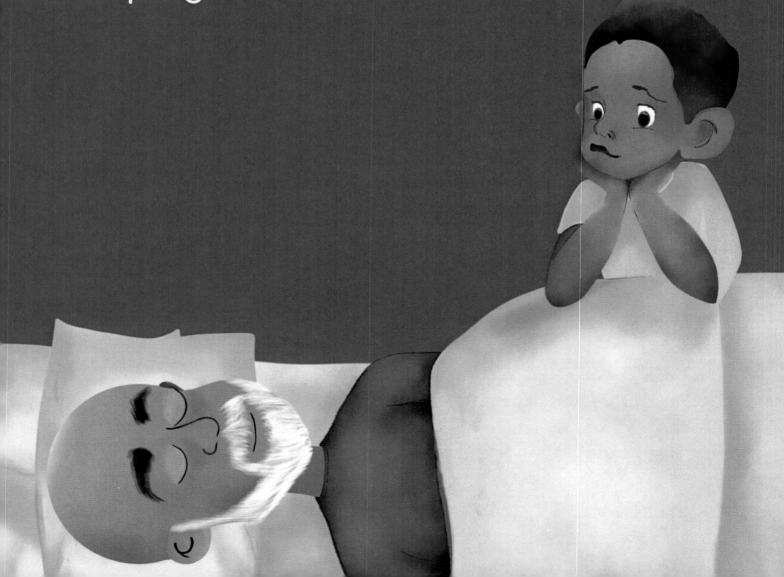

I was not crying because I did not know what to cry about.

Then after what seemed like hours and hours my dad and mom took us home.

My mom was so sad, and I did not understand. I needed to talk to my Gammy, she would tell me what was going on.

We went to Gammy's house every day for about a week to eat dinner and just be with her. There were so many people who came to her house that I knew I would not get a chance to talk to her.

The adults talked for many days, but I did not go into the room where Poppy was because I thought he was still asleep.

A few days later, Gammy and I sat in a chair and she told me that Poppy was gone and was not coming back. What, what does that mean? Poppy went out of town a lot so maybe that is what she meant.

But she said he was not coming back. No, that cannot be, Poppy loved us and would never leave us and not come back.

All that night I thought about Poppy leaving us.

You mean he just got up out of the bed and left us? No, that cannot be right.

So, I got up enough nerve to ask my mom. She said Poppy died.

Those words hit me in the chest like a heavy Velociraptor or a T-Rex and would not get off. I felt them every day.

Sometimes I got really mad and wanted to hit my brother for no reason at all except that maybe those dinosaurs would get off me if I hit him or someone else.

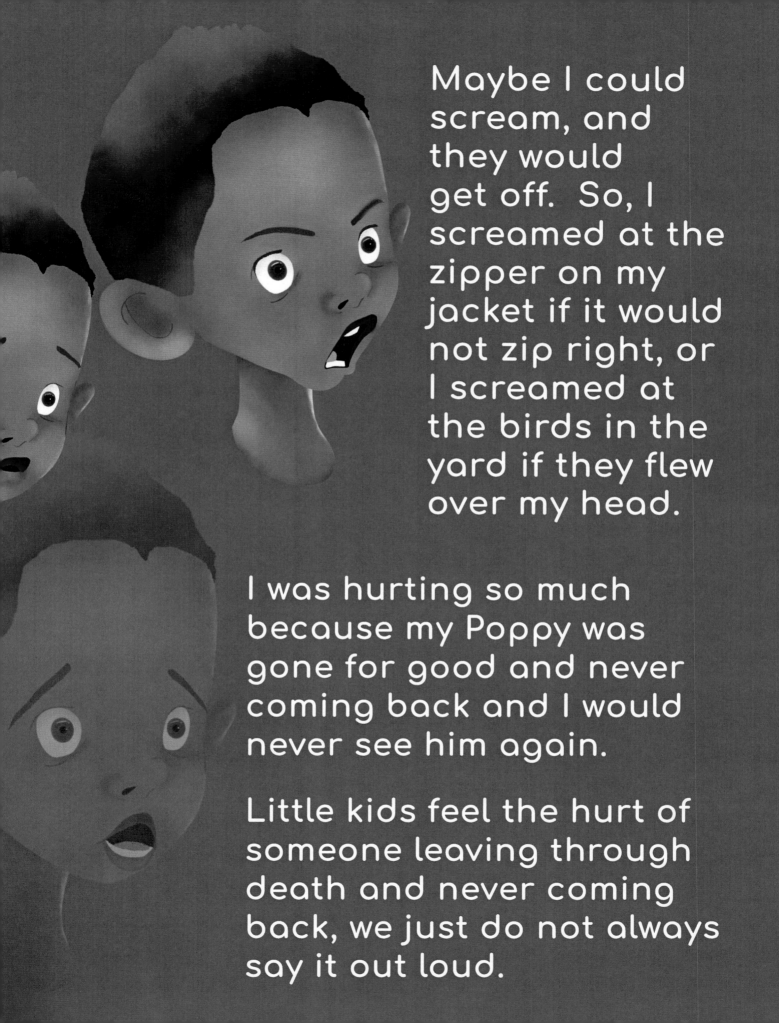

Maybe I could scream, and they would get off. So, I screamed at the zipper on my jacket if it would not zip right, or I screamed at the birds in the yard if they flew over my head.

I was hurting so much because my Poppy was gone for good and never coming back and I would never see him again.

Little kids feel the hurt of someone leaving through death and never coming back, we just do not always say it out loud.

I remember the day that my mom said we were going to the Homegoing service. What is that? Well, some people call it a funeral.

Me and my brother went to Gammy's house and showed her how nice we looked. We had new shirts, pants, and shoes. She thought we looked so nice that she took a picture of us.

We got to ride in a limousine. Wow, that car was long!

A funeral is a time when people come to say nice things about what your loved one did or said.

Boy oh boy, my Poppy had a lot of people coming to say nice things about him.

There were so many people who wanted to talk about Poppy that it took two days!

But I never got to say anything about him. I think everyone thought I was too small to have anything to say.

I did have something to say. I wanted to say that I loved my Poppy and I was waiting for my turn to ride on his motorcycle. I got to sit on it, but I was not big enough to ride with him yet.

I wanted to say that I remember riding in his convertible with the top down. Poppy made me feel big.

I wanted to say that I liked watching TV with him, especially Star Trek.

I wanted to say that I liked looking at his model cars because he had a bunch of them, and we knew not to touch them. His office had a lot of neat things that we could only look at, but I liked looking.

I was only four years old when my Poppy left us, because he was sick and in pain, but I still remember and love him.

When someone is in your heart that means you remember them, and you think about them. You think about something they did or something they said, or something they liked to eat.

Even though my Poppy was a pastor, to me he was the horse I rode round the family room.

Gammy says that memories are wonderful things to help you get through missing someone, and they help you keep the person alive in your heart. We have lots of pictures of Poppy and that will help me tell my little sisters who he was.

I plan to tell them things about our Poppy so that even though they did not get to meet him, I can help them know how great our Poppy was.

I can't see him, but I can still feel him.